W9-BWU-659

South
Downs

river

POINTS 2.0

BOOK LEVEL 4.6

TEST # 511495

Ben's
house

Button
found here

Sky
found here

Chicken coop

Farmyard

Calf barn

Holly
found here

Jasmine's
house

Lucky
born here

8/21

JF Peters
Peters, Helen.
A goat called Willow

urner's farm →

Jasmine Green Rescues
A Goat
Called Willow

Read all the books in the
Jasmine Green Rescues series

Jasmine Green Rescues
A Goat
Called Willow

Helen Peters
illustrated by Ellie Snowdon

WALKER BOOKS

Text copyright © 2018 by Helen Peters
Illustrations copyright © 2018 by Ellie Snowdon

First US edition 2021
First published by Nosy Crow (UK) 2018

Library of Congress Catalog Card Number pending
ISBN 978-1-5362-1029-3 (hardcover)
ISBN 978-1-5362-1605-9 (paperback)

20 21 22 23 24 25 LBM 10 9 8 7 6 5 4 3 2 1

Printed in Melrose Park, IL, USA

This book was typeset in Bembo.
The illustrations were done in pencil with a digital wash overlay.

Walker Books US
a division of
Candlewick Press
99 Dover Street
Somerville, Massachusetts 02144

www.walkerbooksus.com

To my brother, Mark
HP

For my dad
ES

1
Kid For Sale

"You can buy yourselves a souvenir, or spend it on fairground rides and cotton candy, whichever you like," said Mom, handing some money to Jasmine and her best friend, Tom. "Meet me back here at four o'clock, OK?"

"Wow, thanks, Mom," said Jasmine, looking in delight at the money.

"Thank you very much, Dr. Singh," said Tom.

"Can me and Ben go off on our own, too?" asked Jasmine's little brother, Manu.

"Certainly not," said Mom. "You two need to stay with me."

"But that's not fair!"

"When you're ten, you can go off without me," said Mom. "Jasmine wasn't allowed to wander around the sheep fair on her own when she was six."

"Come on, Sky," said Jasmine, giving her sheepdog's leash a little shake. "Let's go and see the sheep."

The Fenton Sheep Fair was held every year in a big field on a farm in the South Downs. There was a fairground, a craft tent, and all sorts of stalls selling food and drinks. But, for Jasmine and Tom, the main attraction was the sheep.

They made their way to the top of the field. Here, several rows of pens had been built from metal rails, with walkways between the rows. Each pen contained a small group of sheep, all washed and groomed to perfection.

A voice crackled over the sound system. "The next class to be judged will be Southdown ewe lambs. Could all entrants make their way to the show ring now, please."

"You should have entered Lucky," said Tom.

Lucky was Jasmine's pet lamb. His mother had died when he was born, and Jasmine had bottle-fed him until he was old enough to live on grass.

"I wanted to enter him," said Jasmine. "But Dad's too busy with the cows to come to the fair, and Mom was working this morning."

Jasmine's dad was a farmer and her mom was a farm vet, so they were always busy looking after animals or doing office work.

"Let's go and see the lambs in the ring," said Tom. "I bet none of them are as cute as Lucky."

They walked between the pens toward the show ring. In some of the pens, farmers were brushing their sheep's woolly coats. One woman was oiling her sheep's hooves to make them shine.

"Oh, look!" said Jasmine. She hurried along the walkway to get a closer look. "Oh, it's so cute!"

In the far corner of the farthest pen sat a beautiful baby goat. Its coat was mainly brown, with patches of black and white on its legs and back, and a white blaze down the middle of its face. As Jasmine and Tom leaned over the gate, the kid greeted them with a high-pitched bleat.

"Oh, you're so sweet," said Jasmine. "Come here so I can stroke you."

"It's a girl," said Tom. "Look, she's for sale."

He pointed to a handwritten notice tied to the bars of the pen.

FEMALE KID FOR SALE

Jasmine's eyes widened. "Oh, I wish we could buy her."

Tom laughed. "Imagine how mad your mom and dad would be if you did."

Jasmine already had six animals of her own, and her parents had told her that she wasn't allowed to have any more. She and Tom planned to run an animal rescue center when they grew up. So

far, they had rescued a runt piglet, a motherless duckling, an abandoned puppy, a rejected kitten, two baby sparrows, and an orphaned lamb.

They had released the sparrows when they were fully grown, and Holly the kitten now belonged to Tom, but Jasmine had persuaded her parents to let her keep Truffle the pig, Button the duck, Lucky the lamb, and Sky the sheepdog. She also had two cats called Toffee and Marmite.

"Anyway," said Tom, noticing a price written in below the sign, "with the money your mom gave us, we could only buy half of her."

The little goat stood up, bleated, and took a few tentative steps toward the children. Jasmine stroked her back.

"Her coat's so soft," she said. "Feel it, Tom. Sorry, little goat. I can't buy you, but I hope you find a lovely home."

"Mind your backs," said a gruff voice behind them.

They turned to see a man leading two sheep

on halters. The children stepped away from the gate so he could open it and take the sheep inside.

"Excuse me," said Jasmine in her politest voice. "Is this your kid?"

He grunted in a tone that Jasmine understood to mean yes.

"She's beautiful," said Jasmine. "How old is she?"

"Four weeks," he said, taking the halter off one of the ewes. "If you're not going to buy her, clear off. I've had enough time-wasters asking pointless questions."

"Actually, I'm thinking about buying her," she said, giving him a look that she hoped made it clear she was a serious farmer about to do a deal.

"Well, don't think about it much longer. I'm heading off shortly."

A flicker of hope rose inside Jasmine. If nobody bought the goat today, maybe she could persuade her parents to let her buy it later.

"What will you do if you don't sell her today?" she asked.

"Shoot her."

"Shoot her!" Jasmine was so shocked that her words came out as a squeal. "No! Why would you do that?"

"The mother just died," he said, "and I don't have time to bottle-feed the kid. I was going to shoot her yesterday, but since I was coming here, I thought I might as well bring her and see if anyone fancied hand-rearing. Seems like nobody else has the time either, though. I'll shoot her as soon as I get back."

Jasmine was suddenly filled with determination. She had no idea how she was going to manage it, but she knew one thing. She wasn't going to allow this tiny animal to be shot.

"We'll buy her," she said.

Tom gave her a worried look.

"We don't have all the money with us now," Jasmine said, "but we can give you half and pay the rest later."

"Where do you live?" he asked.

"Oak Tree Farm. In Westcombe."

He looked at her with slightly more respect. "So you're Mike Green's girl."

Jasmine nodded.

"Is your dad here, then?"

"No, but my mom is."

"And they don't mind you buying a goat?"

"Of course not," said Jasmine, crossing her fingers. "They love goats. We can't take her home right now, though. We'll have to get everything ready. Would you be able to deliver her tomorrow?"

"Martin!" called somebody from the other side of the pen. "How are you? Haven't seen you for ages."

The two men started to chat. Tom grabbed Jasmine's sleeve.

"What are you doing?" he whispered.

"What?" said Jasmine innocently. "Mom said we could buy a souvenir. She never said it couldn't be alive."

"You know she won't let you buy her."

"She doesn't need to know," said Jasmine. "I've got enough money saved up."

"But what about—"

"Tom, do you want this beautiful little goat to be killed tonight?"

Tom sighed. "Of course I don't."

"So don't worry about anything else. We'll work it all out later. The only thing that matters right now is that we save her life."

2

It's Not Going to Be Easy

Once they had convinced the farmer, whose name was Mr. Evans, that they were serious about buying the baby goat, they paid him half the money and he agreed to deliver her at ten o'clock the following morning, as he was going to be in the area anyway. Jasmine asked him to drive into the field from the gate that led out to the lane. That way, he wouldn't need to come into the farmyard, and no one else would see him arrive.

"We just saved an animal's life," said Jasmine as they made their way to the show ring.

"I'm glad we spent our money on a goat instead of fairground rides," said Tom.

"We *are* the Animal Rescue Club, after all."

"Exactly," said Jasmine. "When we have our rescue center, this is what we'll be doing all the time."

"What should we call her?" asked Tom.

Jasmine gazed around the field. Her eyes landed on a huge weeping willow tree in the corner.

"What do you think about Willow?" she asked.

"Willow," said Tom. "That's a good name for a goat."

"How are we going to keep her hidden?" asked Jasmine. "She'll need a shed. Goats can't stay outdoors all the time like sheep. They need shelter. But she'll need grass, too, with a fence around it, so . . ."

Tom's eyes lit up. "I know! The field where the sheep are. There's that old chicken run in the corner."

"Oh, yes," said Jasmine. "With the little shed. That will be perfect."

13

"What about when your dad checks the sheep, though?" asked Tom. "He'll see her if she's out in the run."

"He checks them early in the morning and in the evening," said Jasmine, "so she'll be in the shed then. It will all work out fine. We just need to clean out the shed and bed it down. Can you come back to my house after the fair?"

Tom made a face. "No, we're going out to dinner with some friends of my parents who I don't even like."

Jasmine laughed. "Can you come tomorrow morning, then? Dad usually checks the sheep at about half past six, so if you come at eight, he'll be back in the yard and we can go and get the shed ready."

Tom nodded. "I'll tell Mom we're taking Sky for an early walk."

"It's good that Mr. Evans is bringing milk," said Jasmine. "I don't know how we'd have managed to get goat's milk by tomorrow morning."

14

"He's only bringing enough for one day, though," said Tom. "How are we going to afford two liters a day after that? And how are we going to buy it without our parents finding out?"

"Hmm," said Jasmine. "We'll have to come up with a plan."

Tom arrived in the sunlit farmyard before eight o'clock on Sunday morning. Jasmine and Sky were already in the old stable where they kept the bedding for Truffle, Jasmine's pet pig.

"Hey, Tom," called Jasmine. "Come and help me fill these wheelbarrows."

She had trundled two wheelbarrows into the stable. They filled one with sections of a hay bale, and the other with wood shavings.

"Your goat's milk plan worked perfectly," said Tom.

"Really? Oh, that's great. I didn't get a chance to ask my mom last night. She got called out to a foaling."

"Mom was a bit surprised, but when I told her we'd been learning about how healthy goat's milk is, she was really pleased. She even said she'll try switching, too. She's going to get some today."

"I'll ask my mom this morning," said Jasmine as she balanced a broom and a bucket on top of the shavings in her wheelbarrow. She put a bottle of disinfectant, a scrubbing brush, and a shovel in Tom's wheelbarrow. "Right, let's go."

She hitched a backpack onto her shoulders. It contained a lamb's feeding bottle, a dog bowl, and some food she'd taken from the kitchen for a breakfast picnic.

"Mom asked if you want to come to our house for lunch," said Tom.

"Yes, please," said Jasmine. "Then we can heat up Willow's lunchtime milk at your house, too."

They trundled the wheelbarrows across the yard, walking around the back of the buildings so that nobody would see them. But as they were crossing the driveway into Hawthorn Field, Manu came running out of the house.

"Oh, no," muttered Jasmine.

"Where are you going?" Manu asked, looking at the wheelbarrows.

Jasmine thought quickly. "We're cleaning out Truffle's kennel."

Truffle shared a big kennel with Bramble, Dad's springer spaniel. The kennel opened into the orchard so that Truffle could spend her days rooting about under the fruit trees.

"That's not the way to Truffle's kennel," said Manu.

Tom laughed. "Oh, yes. Silly us. We were chatting and we went the wrong way."

"You two are so clueless," said Manu.

"So clueless," agreed Jasmine. "Come on, Sky."

They turned the wheelbarrows around and began to push them toward the orchard. Manu ran off across the yard. Tom and Jasmine paused at the orchard gate until his footsteps faded into the distance. Then they turned the wheelbarrows around again and trundled them into Hawthorn Field.

"It's not going to be easy, keeping this a secret," said Tom.

 18

"At least we've got Truffle and Sky as alibis," said Jasmine.

They walked through Hawthorn Field to the horse paddock. There were no horses there now. Instead, sheep and lambs grazed the lush summer grass. Jasmine's pet lamb, Lucky, was among them. When he saw the children, he bounded across to them, bleating loudly. A condition in his back legs meant he had a very distinctive way of moving, running with his front legs and jumping with his back ones.

Jasmine crouched down to give him a hug. "We've got a new baby coming today, Lucky. This hay is for her, but you can have some, too."

She took a handful of hay from the wheelbarrow. Lucky gobbled it up and trotted back to his friends. Tom and Jasmine pushed their wheelbarrows to the corner of the field, which was fenced off with chicken wire to make a large pen. Jasmine wiggled and pulled at the rusty bolt on the gate until it finally slid back.

"I hope someone cleaned the shed out when they stopped keeping chickens here," she said, "or it will be really gross."

Wrinkling her nose, Jasmine pulled back the bolt on the shed door.

"Oh," said Tom. "Nobody cleaned it out."

A deep layer of chicken dung covered the floor. Insects ran up the walls and spiders' webs hung in the corners.

"At least the dung's dried up," said Jasmine. "It doesn't smell too bad."

She picked up the shovel, and Tom took the hay out of the wheelbarrow to make room for the muck. They cleaned out all the mess and swept the walls and ceiling clear of cobwebs. Then they scrubbed the shed and disinfected it.

"Let's have breakfast while it dries," said Jasmine.

They cleaned their hands with diluted disinfectant and wiped them dry on the back of their jeans. Then they sat on a fallen tree trunk in the middle

of the horse paddock and took out the food from their backpacks. Tom had brought two chocolate chip muffins and two bags of chips. Jasmine had a package of cookies, a carton of orange juice, and two apples. She also had some dog treats for Sky, who sat on the grass beside them as they ate.

"I don't think that fence is secure enough," said Jasmine. "I bet Willow could wriggle under those gaps at the bottom. Goats are really good at escaping."

"We could use tent pegs to pin the wire down," said Tom. "I can go and get ours."

Tom lived in a cottage on the lane that ran along the edge of Oak Tree Farm, so it was easy for him to get home across the fields.

"That's a great idea," said Jasmine.

"I can't believe he's making us pay extra for delivery," said Tom, taking another cookie. "How mean is that?"

Jasmine gasped and clapped her hand to her mouth. "Oh, no!"

"What?"

"I forgot to bring the money. I'll have to run home and get it."

"I'll do the bedding while you're gone," said Tom. "Don't be long."

"I won't." Jasmine looked at her watch. "Willow's arriving in less than an hour. I can't wait!"

3
Who Was That?

Jasmine ran all the way home, Sky bounding ahead of her. The cats were curled up asleep on her bed when she burst into her room, gasping for breath. Marmite opened her eyes and lifted her head inquiringly.

"I've only got a few coins in the whole world now," Jasmine said to her as she pulled all the bills out of her piggy bank. "That's not going to buy much goat's milk, is it? Let's hope Mom falls for the plan like Tom's mom did."

She stuffed the money into her pocket and headed downstairs. From the kitchen came the sound of voices and the smell of bacon frying. Jasmine opened the front door as quietly as she could, hoping to tiptoe out without being noticed.

"Jasmine!" called her mom. "Is that you?"

Jasmine sighed. Why did Mom have to have such ridiculously good hearing?

"Coming," she said.

Dad was cooking breakfast at the big Aga stove. Mom was putting bread into the toaster. Jasmine's seventeen-year-old sister, Ella, was making a pot of tea.

"Where have you been?" Mom asked. "And do you know what's happened to the orange juice? Everyone else swears they haven't drunk it."

"Oh, sorry," said Jasmine. "I was thirsty."

Mom raised her eyebrows. "Well, next time you're thirsty, drink water, not the entire carton of juice that was meant for the whole family."

"Sorry," said Jasmine.

"Come and sit down for breakfast," said Dad.

"Oh, that's OK, I'm not hungry. I'm going to walk Sky."

"You just walked Sky. And you need breakfast."

"I don't have time," said Jasmine. "Tom's here to do some sheepdog training. And I'm really not hungry. Oh, and Mom?"

"Yes?"

"When you go shopping, could you buy goat's milk, please?"

Mom turned to Jasmine, a puzzled frown on her face.

"Goat's milk? What for?"

"Raw goat's milk, it has to be. Not pasteurized. So you'll have to get it at the farm store. If that's OK."

"Why on earth do you want raw goat's milk?"

"We've been learning about how healthy it is. It's much better for you than cow's milk. And it's really good if you have allergies."

"But you don't have allergies."

"I know, but I think I might be getting an allergy to cow's milk. So could you get some? Please?"

"Well, OK, if you're really going to drink it. I was planning to go to the farm store anyway."

"Thanks, Mom. Oh, and I'm going to Tom's for lunch. His mom asked me."

"Remember you need to muck out Truffle's kennel today," said Dad as he lifted the tomatoes out of the pan.

"Oh, yes, I will in a bit."

Manu gave her a puzzled look. "But you just did it."

"Well, I just had a look in there," said Dad, "and it definitely hadn't been done."

"But she was going to do it. Tom and her both had wheelbarrows, with shavings and hay and everything."

"We decided to take Sky for a walk instead," said Jasmine. "We'll muck Truffle out later."

She glanced out of the window just as a dusty gray truck drove into the yard, pulling a livestock trailer.

Oh, no. It was Mr. Evans! How could that have happened? They had specifically told him to come to the gate on the lane. She had to turn him away before anyone else saw.

Trying not to appear panicked, she left the kitchen as casually as she could. As soon as she was out of the back door, she broke into a sprint, waving her arms to attract Mr. Evans's attention. He finished reversing the truck and braked in the middle of the yard.

"Morning," he said. "Is your dad around? Where does he want this kid?"

As Jasmine was giving him directions to the field, the garden gate rattled open and Mom came out.

"I'll meet you in the field," Jasmine whispered to Mr. Evans. "Tom's there already."

"Can I help you?" called Mom.

"No, it's fine," Jasmine called back. "He's just going."

She turned to Mr. Evans again.

"Go, now!" she whispered. "Quickly!"

Giving her a look that made it obvious he thought she was a bit odd, he revved the engine and drove out of the yard.

"Who was that," asked Mom, "and why did you come out to talk to him?"

Jasmine shrugged. "I saw him from the window and he looked lost, so I gave him directions, that's all. I need to go and do Sky's training now. Tom's waiting. Bye!"

She strode off through the orchard. Glancing back, she saw that Mom was still watching her. Only after she climbed over the gate did Mom turn and walk back to the house. As soon as she was out of sight, Jasmine broke into a sprint.

 30

4

One Mischievous Little Goat

Mr. Evans's truck was parked next to Willow's pen. Jasmine hurried over as the farmer opened the trailer.

The little goat, who looked even smaller and cuter than Jasmine remembered, bleated pleadingly from the far corner of the trailer.

"Oh, she looks so frightened and confused," said Jasmine. "Can I go in?"

Mr. Evans nodded. Jasmine walked in. Willow bleated piteously and pressed herself farther into the corner. Jasmine reached toward her and

Willow bolted past her outstretched arms. Mr. Evans caught her as she tried to run out. He handed her to Tom.

"She's a bit skittish," he said.

"That's all right," said Jasmine, stroking the little goat and feeling her heart beating fast under her warm coat. "We're going to handle her a lot. She'll calm down soon."

Willow bleated, but she didn't struggle.

"She's so soft and warm," said Tom.

"She's had her first round of vaccinations," said Mr. Evans. "She'll need booster shots in three or four weeks' time."

"Right," said Jasmine. She could tell that Tom was giving her a worried look, so she avoided his gaze. How were they going to get Willow vaccinated in secret?

Mr. Evans looked at the pen.

"Should be high enough to keep out foxes," he said, "but I'd shut her in at night, to be on the safe side."

 32

Jasmine looked at Tom in horror. She hadn't even thought about foxes.

"We'll shut her in the shed every evening," said Tom. "Will she be all right in the daytime, though?"

"Should be," Mr. Evans said. "You'll need to make that fence more secure at the bottom, though, or she'll be out in no time. All right, here's the movement form. Give that to your dad so he can fill in his part."

He held out an official-looking form. To Jasmine's horror, it was several pages long. Buying farm animals was a lot more complicated than she'd thought.

"OK," she said, trying to sound casual. "Thanks."

She stared in dismay at the form. The blank boxes had headings like DESTINATION CPH OR SLAUGHTERHOUSE NO. and ADDITIONAL FCI. What did it all mean? How were they going to fill it in without any help? And where did they have to send it?

"Don't forget," said Mr. Evans as Jasmine folded the form and stuffed it in her pocket. "It needs to be sent off within three days."

"Right," said Jasmine.

The farmer took a lemonade bottle filled with milk from the truck and handed it to Jasmine. "That'll be enough for today," he said. "She's been fed this morning. I just need you to pay the balance and I'll be on my way."

Jasmine pulled the money from her pocket. He took it, nodded, and returned to his truck. Without another word, he closed the door, started the engine, and bumped off across the field.

"He didn't even say goodbye to Willow," said Tom as they watched him drive away.

"Grumpy old farmer," said Jasmine. She kissed the goat's head. "You're ours now, Willow. And you're going to have a lovely life with us."

Tom stroked Willow's face. "I'll run home and get the tent pegs," he said. "We don't want you

34

getting out, Willow. And we definitely don't want foxes getting in."

He set off across the field. Jasmine sat on the grass to wait for him, with Willow snuggled in her lap. Jasmine stroked her soft ears. Willow nibbled Jasmine's fingers. After a few minutes, the little goat curled up and fell asleep.

"Sorry I can't help," said Jasmine when Tom returned with a handful of tent pegs, "but I've got a sleeping kid on my lap."

"Can you imagine?" said Tom, kneeling on

the grass. "If we hadn't bought her, she'd be dead by now."

He pulled the bottom of the fence down, hooked the tent peg through the wire, and pushed it into the ground. Willow opened her eyes and turned her head to watch him. Tom shuffled along to work on another part of the fence. Willow scrambled to her feet, her hard little hooves pressing into Jasmine's thighs. Suddenly, she leaped from Jasmine's lap and landed squarely on Tom's back.

Jasmine burst out laughing as Tom squealed in surprise.

"Willow, what are you doing?" he cried. "Get off my back!"

Willow turned around on his back, then leaped through the air onto the low roof of the shed.

"Wow, that's amazing," said Jasmine. "She's like a gymnast."

Willow ran around on the roof, sniffing at the edges, and then sprang back down to the ground.

36

"Imagine if we could enter her in the agility class at the festival," said Tom.

The town festival was happening in a few weeks' time. It was held on the town green, and the preparations had been going on for months. There were all sorts of stalls and competitions. Jasmine's mom, who loved gardening, was planning to enter several of the flower and vegetable events. But the highlight of the festival for Tom and Jasmine was the pet show. Tom was going to enter his guinea pigs in the small animal event. Jasmine had wanted to enter Sky in the obedience event, but Dad had said he wasn't quite ready yet.

"Willow would be way better than all the dogs

in the agility class," said Jasmine. "It's a shame we have to keep her a secret."

They looked at Willow as she sniffed around the bottom of the fence. When she found a section where the wire wasn't securely fixed to the ground, she began to nudge at it with her head. They watched, fascinated, as she pushed the wire up with the top of her head, then got down on her tummy and started to wriggle underneath the fence. Jasmine went over and grabbed her.

"Guess we'd better stick a tent peg in there," said Tom, taking another peg out of his backpack.

Jasmine held out her hand. "I'll do some, too."

She set Willow down on the ground. The goat started to nibble at her jeans.

"Watch out," called Tom in alarm. "She's eating paper."

Jasmine looked down to see Willow nibbling a corner of the bill of sale that was sticking out of her pocket. She gave a yelp of dismay. "No, Willow! Stop that!"

With a jerk of her head, Willow pulled the form out of Jasmine's pocket.

The paper was fast disappearing inside her mouth.

"No, Willow!"

Jasmine pulled the goat's jaws apart and fished out the form. One corner was chewed off and the paper was crumpled and soggy in places, but most of the writing was still readable.

"Wow, we're really going to have to keep an eye on you," said Jasmine, kissing the top of her head. "You are one mischievous little goat."

5
Discovered Already

By the time Tom and Jasmine had finished fixing the fence, Willow had worn herself out with all the leaping around. They introduced her to her new shed, and after nosing around for a bit and eating some of the hay and grain, she snuggled down in her soft hay bed. They left her sleeping peacefully and walked to Tom's house for lunch.

Jasmine frowned as she saw a familiar car parked on the lane outside Tom's cottage.

"What's my mom doing here? Is she spying on me?"

"Oh, I think my mom's giving her some clothes I've grown out of, for Manu," said Tom.

As they walked up the path, they could hear their mothers' voices through the open kitchen window.

"They do get some funny ideas, don't they?" Miss Mel was saying. "Tom's just randomly decided he wants to drink goat's milk instead of cow's milk. Only raw goat's milk, too, would you believe?"

Tom and Jasmine stopped walking and shot each other fearful glances. Were they going to be found out?

"How strange," said Mom. "Jasmine's decided exactly the same thing. She gave me a whole lecture about the health benefits of raw goat's milk. Said they'd been learning about it. Their teacher clearly has a lot to answer for."

"Well, I wish I was half as persuasive as she is,"

said Miss Mel. "Tom clearly pays a lot more attention to Miss Hamblin's advice then he ever does to mine."

"Oh, they all do," said Mom. She started talking about something Manu had said the other day, and Tom and Jasmine stopped listening.

"Phew," said Tom as they walked into the house. "Thank goodness they didn't suspect anything."

As soon as they had eaten and Tom's mom was safely out of the way, they heated up a pan of Mr. Evans's goat's milk, poured it into the feeding bottle, and walked back to the horse paddock. As they climbed over the gate, they could see Willow in her pen. She was standing at the fence on her hind legs, her front hooves planted on the chicken wire, watching the sheep.

"Oh, poor Willow," said Jasmine. "She looks lonely."

"What if we let her out for a bit to play with the lambs?" asked Tom. "Just while we're here, I mean."

42

"As long as she comes back when we call her," said Jasmine. "We can't risk her running off."

"Maybe we'd better wait a few days," said Tom, "until she really knows us."

"Willow!" called Jasmine. "We're back!"

Willow turned her head. Seeing the children, she ran to the gate of her pen, bleating and wiggling her tail. As Jasmine opened the gate, Willow nuzzled against her and rubbed her head against Jasmine's leg. Then, as if to show that she loved them both, she skipped across to Tom and rubbed her head against his leg, too.

"She's bonded with us already," said Tom, stroking her soft neck.

"Or she's hungry," said Jasmine. "Maybe she can smell the milk."

She took the bottle from her backpack and held it out to the little goat. Willow clamped the teat between her jaws and sucked enthusiastically. She finished the milk in less than a minute and would have carried on sucking at the empty bottle if

Jasmine hadn't slipped her fingers into her mouth and pulled the teat out.

"Let's see if she comes when we call her," said Tom. "If she does, then maybe we could let her out for a bit."

He walked to the other side of the pen.

"Willow!" he called.

Willow galloped across to him.

"Good girl, Willow," he said, stroking her flank.

"Willow!" called Jasmine. "Come here, Willow!"

Willow galloped back to Jasmine and rubbed her head against her jeans.

"Do you want to go out and play with the lambs?" asked Jasmine.

Tom opened the gate and walked into the field. "Here, Willow!" he called.

Willow bounded into the sheep field, kicking up her hind legs and taking enthusiastic sideways leaps. A group of sheep was sitting peacefully under a tree at the edge of the paddock. Willow leaped onto the broad woolly back of the nearest ewe. The sheep took absolutely no notice.

"Do you think they even feel it?" asked Tom as Willow sprang off the ewe's back onto the back of another sheep.

"Wow!" exclaimed somebody behind them.

Tom and Jasmine whipped their heads around. Standing a few yards behind them were Manu and Ben, staring in delight as the ewe trotted away with Willow still standing on her back, balanced like a circus performer.

Jasmine's heart sank. She couldn't believe it. They'd been discovered already!

She scowled at her brother. "What are you doing here?"

"Looking for you," said Manu. "I knew you were doing something secret. You said you were going to clean out Truffle this morning, but you didn't clean her out, so you must have been going somewhere else with those wheelbarrows. And then you said you were going to take Sky for a walk, but you'd just taken him for a walk. So when Ben came, I told him you were acting suspiciously."

"So we decided to spy on you," said Ben. "It was really easy to find you. We're very good spies."

"How come you've got a goat?" asked Manu. "He's so cool. Where did you get him? Mom and Dad said you couldn't have any more animals. Is that why you're keeping him secretly?"

"It's a her, not a him," said Jasmine. "She's called Willow. We got her at the sheep fair. Her mother

47

died and her owner was going to shoot her. So we bought her."

Manu's eyes widened even more. "That's why you asked Mom to buy goat's milk!"

"Yes," said Jasmine. "But you can't tell Mom and Dad. They might make me give her back, and then she'd get shot."

Manu thought for a moment. Then he said, "OK. But only if you let me share her."

"What do you mean, share her?" asked Jasmine warily.

"I want to teach her tricks," said Manu.

Ben's face lit up. "We could build her an obstacle course!"

"Yes!" said Manu. "We can use old tires and planks and stuff."

"You can't," said Jasmine. "Dad will see it when he comes to check the sheep."

"But he'll see Willow, too," said Manu.

"No, we're keeping her in that pen," said Jasmine, pointing to it, "and we've cleaned out the shed for her. She'll be in the shed when Dad checks the sheep."

Suddenly, Tom laughed. Jasmine looked at him. He pointed across the field. "Look! She's made a whole gang of friends!"

Willow was bounding around the edge of the field with Lucky and a few other lambs. As the children watched, they all jumped over a fallen tree branch together, like horses running neck and neck in a race.

"We definitely need to make her an obstacle

course," said Manu. "We'll tell Dad it's for the lambs. That's not a lie. It is for them, too."

"Let's go and get the stuff for it," said Ben.

The boys started running back toward the farmyard.

"Wait!" called Jasmine. They stopped and turned around.

"You can't tell anyone about her," said Jasmine. "Not even your friends at school, OK? It's really serious. If Mom and Dad find out and make me send her back, she'll be killed. Do you understand?"

The boys nodded solemnly. "We swear," said Manu.

They galloped off across the field. Jasmine and Tom watched their retreating backs in silence. Then they looked at each other anxiously.

"Do you think we can trust them?" asked Tom.

Jasmine sighed. "I don't know. I think they'll try to keep it secret, but they're only six. If they get excited, they might forget and blurt out everything. Let's just really hope they don't."

6
How Did You Find Us?

Willow loved her obstacle course. She and the more adventurous lambs played on it for hours that afternoon. When it was time for her to be shut in for the night, she was so exhausted that she was perfectly happy to be picked up and carried into the shed.

"We should do that bill of sale tonight," said Tom. "Mr. Evans said it has to be sent off within three days."

Jasmine made a face. She would cheerfully do

whatever it took to look after her animals, but filling in a scary-looking form was a whole different matter.

"Let's have a look at it," said Tom. "I'm sure we can figure it out."

Jasmine took the crumpled form out of her pocket and handed it to him. She sat on the shed floor, stroking the sleepy little goat in her lap, as Tom frowned in silent concentration over the blank boxes and columns.

"It's not as bad as it looks," he said eventually. "Mr. Evans has filled in most of it. The only section I can't do is this one."

He held out the form, running his finger under the words "Destination CPH or Slaughterhouse No." Next to the words was a row of blank boxes.

"I have no idea what that means," he said, "but Mr. Evans has written a long number in the 'Departure CPH' boxes at the top, so I guess the 'Destination CPH' must be a number your dad

has. But how are we going to find that out without him getting suspicious?"

Jasmine thought for a moment. Then she remembered the conversation they had overheard that morning between her mom and Tom's.

"I think I might know a way," she said. "I'll try to find out tonight."

Tom and Jasmine had recently started walking to school together. On Monday morning, Tom was already waiting at the top of the driveway as Jasmine came around the bend. She broke into a run.

"Did it!" she called triumphantly, waving an envelope. "CPH number all filled in."

"Oh, excellent," said Tom. "How did you get it?"

"I said we're doing a school project on farming," said Jasmine. "I told Dad that Miss Hamblin had asked us to find out what a CPH number was. Then I asked him if I could see his."

"So what is a CPH number?"

"It stands for County/Parish/Holding number," said Jasmine proudly as they walked along Pond Lane. "It's basically an identification number. Every farm has one. He didn't suspect a thing. They just think we're learning about farming, same as with the goat's milk."

Tom made a face. "I had to have goat's milk on my cereal this morning. I was trying to save it all for Willow, but my mom put it on the table for breakfast. It's disgusting. Have you tried it?"

Jasmine shook her head. "I used some of ours to feed Willow this morning, so Mom thought I'd drunk it. I didn't want to waste any, so I just had toast for breakfast."

"You're lucky," said Tom. "It tastes like—"

"Shh," said Jasmine, grabbing his arm. "What was that?"

"What?"

Jasmine was looking back toward the farm. "I'm sure I heard Willow bleating."

"All this way from her field? You couldn't have."

"Not from her field. From close by."

And then it came again, loud and clear. Willow's high-pitched bleat. Around the corner of the lane, the little goat appeared, racing toward them. She ran up and nuzzled their legs, nibbling at their pants.

"Oh, my goodness," said Jasmine, picking Willow up and kissing her head. "How did you find us?"

"How did she get out?" said Tom. "I checked all around the bottom of the fence last night."

"She must have worked her way out. Oh, Willow, I wish you could come to school with us, but you really can't. And Mom will be driving past with Manu soon."

"Oh, what a lovely little kid!"

They turned to see the kind, twinkling face of a little old lady in a tweed skirt and a hand-knitted purple cardigan. She was carrying a wicker basket.

Jasmine recognized her as Mrs. Thomas, one of the nicest of the many people who would stop and talk to her mom about their animals when they were shopping in the town.

"Hello, Mrs. Thomas," she said.

"Hello, Jasmine. What a beautiful little goat. Is she yours?"

"Yes," said Jasmine, setting her down on the ground. "She's called Willow."

"What a perfect name. She's lovely. Aren't you, Willow?"

She stroked Willow's back. Willow pushed her nose into the basket. Mrs. Thomas laughed.

"You're just like my Poppy, aren't you?" she said. "Always looking for something to eat."

"Oh, do you have goats?" asked Jasmine.

"Only two now. I used to have several. I sold the milk and cheese to the farm store for years. When my husband died, I reduced the herd, but I kept Poppy and Bluebell. They're such lovely company, aren't they? I couldn't imagine life without goats around."

Jasmine heard a car coming along the lane. "That might be Mom," she said. "We need to take her back."

"She escaped from her pen," Tom explained.

"Oh, dear," said Mrs. Thomas. "They do enjoy escaping."

"If you see my mom, would you mind not mentioning it to her?" asked Jasmine. "She doesn't quite know we have a goat yet."

Mrs. Thomas looked a bit bewildered by this, but she said, "Of course. I won't breathe a word."

The children took the shortcut back across the fields, with Willow bounding beside them, delighted at the game.

"No more escaping, Willow," said Jasmine as they led her into her pen. "Do you understand? You've got plenty of food and water."

"Here's where she got out," said Tom. He pointed to the bottom of the fence, where a section of chicken wire had been pushed up to create a gap. "She managed to pull the whole peg out."

"Do you think we should shut her in the shed?" asked Jasmine as Tom pushed the peg back into the ground.

Tom screwed up his nose. "It wouldn't be very nice to keep her locked in all day."

"Well, make sure you behave yourself," said Jasmine, kissing Willow's head. "We'll come and see you as soon as we get home."

7

A Goat in the Playground

As Tom and Jasmine ran back across the fields, red-faced and out of breath, Mom's car appeared on the driveway. They ducked down behind the hedge until it was out of sight.

"She didn't see us, did she?" asked Jasmine.

"I don't think so," said Tom. He glanced at his watch. "We're going to be so late."

When they arrived at school, the only person on the playground was Mr. Morrison, the grumpy custodian, who was watering his beloved window boxes. Mr. Morrison hated children, but he loved flowers.

Tom and Jasmine signed in at the office and joined their class as unobtrusively as possible, slipping into their seats and settling down to their math worksheets.

The first few questions were easy, but then Jasmine came to one that she didn't know how to do. She chewed on the end of her pencil and gazed out of the window. Mr. Morrison had finished watering the plants, and the only sound from the empty playground was the dripping of water from the windowsills onto the ground.

And then, on the sidewalk outside the school fence, appeared a little animal.

Willow.

Jasmine froze. For a few seconds, she just stared, not moving, not thinking, not even breathing. Then her brain began to work frantically. What was she going to do? How was she going to get Willow back to the farm without anyone noticing?

She wished she could talk to Tom, but he was bent over his work on the other side of the classroom, completely oblivious to the terrible problem outside.

Jasmine turned back to the window. Oh, no! Willow had her head through the fence. Now she was wriggling her shoulders through. And her front legs. And her back legs.

She was on the playground.

As Jasmine stared, frozen in panic, Willow gave a little shake of her head and looked around at her new surroundings.

Which fun activity should I start with? she seemed to be thinking.

She trotted over to the play equipment. She jumped onto the seesaw and ran along it. As she crossed the center point, it tipped down and she jumped off in surprise. She gazed at the strange new object. Then she stood on the other end and walked up the slope. It tipped again as she crossed the center point, and she jumped off again. She nibbled experimentally at a shrub in the flower bed.

Suddenly, Jasmine decided on a course of action. She would ask to go to the bathroom, and then she would sneak out to the playground and take Willow home. It would take ages, and she had no idea what excuse she could give for being out of class for so long, but she would think of something.

She put up her hand.

"Miss Hamblin, please may I go to the bathroom?"

The teacher sighed. "Jasmine, you've only just arrived. Can't you wait until break time?"

Jasmine was about to reply when there came a shout from the next table.

"Look, there's a dog on the swing!"

Everybody jumped up and ran to the windows.

"It's not a dog, it's a baby goat!" said Marco.

"Aw, it's so cute!" said Aisha.

The classroom exploded into a hubbub of excited chatter. Jasmine stayed frozen in her chair for a second. Then she, too, got up, realizing it would look odd if she didn't.

"Back to your seats, everyone, and stop talking!" ordered Miss Hamblin. Nobody moved.

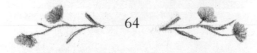

Everyone was laughing and exclaiming at Willow as she leaped from side to side of the big tire swing.

Jasmine caught Tom's eye across the crowd of children pressing their faces to the glass. He looked as panicked as she felt.

Miss Hamblin came to the window. "Wow, it really is a baby goat," she said.

Willow jumped off the swing and trotted over to a sweater that was lying by the see-saw. The class laughed as she sniffed it and started to nibble at the buttons.

"That's my sweater!" cried Bella Bradley. "That goat's eating my sweater!"

 65

"I need to get the custodian," said Miss Hamblin, and she opened the door that led onto the playground. All the children followed her out. Willow looked up from the sweater and bleated.

"That is such a cool goat," said Harry. "I want one."

Tom found Jasmine at the back of the crowd. "What are we going to do?" he whispered.

Jasmine didn't reply. She had absolutely no idea what to do.

"If Willow sees us and comes over to us," Tom whispered, "everyone will know she's ours, and they'll call our parents."

Jasmine pictured the scene that would play out when her parents were called in. She felt sick.

Willow abandoned the sweater and trotted over to the school building. She started to nibble at the bright-red flowers in the classroom window box, just as the custodian appeared with Miss Hamblin.

Mr. Morrison gasped in fury. Willow looked up,

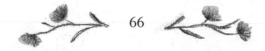

a flower in her mouth, and ran toward him. Miss Hamblin bent down to grab Willow, but the little goat swerved out of her reach and jumped onto a low branch of a big tree that stood at the corner of the building. From that branch, she leaped onto a higher one, and then a higher one again.

"That's amazing," breathed Julia in awe.

"I could do that," said Sonny.

"No, you couldn't."

"I easily could."

As the argument continued, Willow jumped from the tree onto the flat roof of the school. She pranced happily across the roof.

"What if it falls?" cried Zara.

"Goats don't fall," said Rishi. "They're the best climbers in the world."

"Will he just jump down?" asked Patrick.

"Are you going to call the fire department, Miss Hamblin?" asked Sophie.

At that moment, the bell rang for break. From around the corner of the building tumbled a

gaggle of small children. The younger children were coming out to play. And there, right in the middle of them, was Manu.

The younger children followed the gaze of the crowd staring up at the roof. When they saw Willow, there were gasps of amazement and peals of laughter.

Then, above all the other voices in the play-ground, one voice sounded loud and clear.

"Willow!" called Manu. "Willow, what are you doing here?"

Everyone turned to look at Manu. Miss Hamblin tried to hush the crowd.

"Is this your goat, Manu?" she asked him.

Manu shook his head. "She's my sister's goat," he said. "She belongs to Jasmine."

8
We'll Talk About This Later

Jasmine and Tom stood on the playground, two silent, unmoving figures in the swirling sea of children, as Miss Hamblin walked into the building to phone Jasmine's parents. Jasmine's throat was so constricted that she could hardly breathe.

"Why on earth didn't you say the goat belonged to you?" Miss Hamblin had asked her. "You could have caught her right away and it would have been a lot less trouble."

Less trouble for you, perhaps, Jasmine thought. *But*

I'm in more trouble right now than you could possibly imagine, and nothing on earth could make it any better.

Miss Hamblin reappeared as the bell rang for the end of break. As the children lined up to return to their classrooms, she came over to Jasmine.

"I've just had a very awkward phone conversation with your father," she said. "He says you don't have a goat."

She looked at Jasmine, obviously waiting for an answer. Jasmine looked at the ground.

After an excruciating pause, Miss Hamblin said, "Are you going to tell me what's going on here?"

Still Jasmine said nothing.

In a more gentle tone, Miss Hamblin said, "Jasmine, I know that Manu is quite an excitable little boy. Did he perhaps get a bit carried away and say this goat belonged to you?"

Jasmine glanced up at the teacher. Here was a glimmer of hope. She could shift all the blame onto Manu and claim just to be the protective big sister who had backed up a six-year-old's boastful lie.

"You need to tell me the truth, Jasmine," said Miss Hamblin. "If it's not yours, we need to phone the police. They can trace the owner from the goat's ear tag."

"No!" said Jasmine. "Don't do that."

"Why not?"

Jasmine looked at Tom. He shrugged. There was no option left but to tell the truth.

"Willow does belong to me," she said. "But my parents don't exactly know about her yet."

Miss Hamblin stared at Jasmine, her eyes very wide. "I see," she said eventually. "Well, I think now might be the time to tell them, don't you? You'd better go to the office and tell Mrs. Cresswell that you need to make a phone call."

Dad didn't say much on the phone. But that was no comfort to Jasmine. She knew that both he and Mom would have plenty to say later.

He agreed, in a not very good-tempered way, to come and collect Willow from school.

Jasmine and Tom were allowed to go and call her down from the roof. But when they got outside, Willow wasn't on the roof anymore. The playground was empty again, except for the furious custodian, who was glaring up at the big tree next to the hall. Rustling sounds came from the canopy.

"Willow!" called Jasmine. "Willow!"

The canopy rustled even more. Willow jumped nimbly from branch to branch until, with a final leap, she landed on the ground and ran to Jasmine, who knelt down and hugged her.

The custodian gave Jasmine and Tom a filthy look. "Vandalizing school property," he said.

"Destroying my geraniums. You'd better not let it loose again, or—"

"There's Jasmine's dad," said Tom.

Dad's expression was grim as he strode across the playground, although Jasmine thought she saw it soften a little as he looked at Willow. He scooped her up and held her under his arm.

"I'll put her in a cowshed for the time being," he said, "and we'll talk about this when you get home."

Mom and Dad were furious.

"How could you?" said Mom. "How could you do it? Buying that poor goat and keeping it secretly. Deceiving us and lying to us, and then letting it escape and follow you to school. Making us look like complete fools because we didn't even know our own daughter was keeping a pet goat. I thought you were becoming more responsible, and then you go and do this."

"You just couldn't resist having another animal,

could you?" said Dad. "So you lied to us to get your own way."

"No!" said Jasmine. "It wasn't like that. I wasn't going to buy her, I promise."

"And yet you did."

"Only because she would have been killed otherwise. I couldn't let her die."

"What do you mean, she would have been killed?" asked Dad.

"Her mother had died—that's why Mr. Evans was selling her—and he was going to take her home and shoot her because nobody wanted her. That's why I bought her."

Mom took a deep breath.

"I can see that that would have been very upsetting," she said, "but you should have told me about it at the fair, not bought her behind my back."

"But if I'd told you, you still wouldn't have let me buy her, would you?"

"You still should have told me," said Mom.

"You need to be honest with us, Jas. Otherwise how can we trust you with anything?"

"That's not fair. You know you can trust me. I only lied to save her life."

"Mr. Evans should never have sold a goat to a child without speaking to her parents first anyway," said Mom. "It's completely irresponsible. I hope you told him that on the phone, Michael."

"Of course I did," said Dad.

"You called him?" asked Jasmine. "What did he say?"

"He said he'll take her back into his herd as soon as she's weaned," said Dad.

"No!" cried Jasmine. "She's attached to me now. She won't want to go back into a milking herd."

Dad's expression hardened. "It's not your choice, Jasmine. You bought an animal without permission. It's not even legal to bring an animal onto a farm like that. There are forms that need to be filled out, you know. Otherwise you're breaking the law."

"I know that," said Jasmine. "We already filled out the bill of sale."

Her parents stared at her.

"So that's why you wanted to know my CPH number," said Dad.

"Exactly."

"Well, good. Now you'll have all the information you need when you have to fill out another form to send her back."

"But I paid for her. She's mine."

"After what you've put us through today," said Mom, "you can count yourself lucky that you'll have her for another four weeks. After that, she'll be fully weaned, and then she's going straight back to where she came from."

9

Everybody Loves Surprises

"Four weeks until she has to go," said Jasmine to Tom as they walked to school the next morning. "That means four weeks to persuade Mom and Dad that we should keep her."

"I was looking up stuff about goats last night," said Tom, "and it said they're good to keep in a field with sheep because they eat weeds that sheep don't eat, so they're really helpful to farmers."

"We need tons of facts like that," said Jasmine, "to prove to them that she should stay."

"Ooh," said Tom, his eyes lighting up. "We should enter her in the agility class at the festival. That's in three weeks. If she wins, your parents will be so proud that they'll let you keep her."

"She'll definitely win," said Jasmine. "She'll be way better than all the dogs. And there's never been a goat in the agility competition before."

"Will they let you take her, though?"

Jasmine made a face. "Probably not. But we could enter her anyway."

"Secretly? Won't they get mad when they find out?"

"It's not exactly a secret," said Jasmine, "because we want them to find out when they see her in the show, don't we? It's more of a surprise than a secret. And everybody loves surprises."

That evening, Jasmine began researching dog-training techniques on the internet. She discovered that animals don't wear leashes in competitions, so the first thing to do was to teach Willow some basic obedience commands. Luckily, Jasmine knew about obedience training from working with Sky, and Willow was a quick and enthusiastic student.

Once Willow had mastered the commands of Sit, Stay, Come, and Down, Jasmine began to teach her agility. She and Tom altered Manu and Ben's obstacle course to turn it into an agility course similar to the one at last year's town festival. Every day for the next three weeks, they practiced for the competition.

"She's done so well," said Tom on the day before the festival. "I bet she'll be better than all the dogs."

"What if she freaks out at the competition, though?" asked Jasmine. "She's not used to being around lots of dogs. And there'll be so many people, too. What if she just forgets everything and freezes? That's not going to make Mom and Dad want to keep her, is it?"

On the morning of the town festival, after Mom had prepared her best fruits and vegetables for the flower and produce show, she and Jasmine walked to the local farm store to buy bread for lunch and goat's milk for Willow.

"Oh, no," said Jasmine as they reached the parking lot. "That's Mr. Morrison's car."

"Who's Mr. Morrison?"

"Our horrible custodian."

"Oh, him," said Mom. "He always wins the trophies at the show."

"I bet he still looks angry even when he's winning trophies," said Jasmine.

As they entered the shop, Mr. Morrison plunked a pot of parsley and a pot of thyme down on the counter.

"Just that, is it?" asked Lily, the cheerful farmer's daughter who worked in the store.

"Of course it's just that," snapped Mr. Morrison. "If I wanted to buy anything else, don't you think I would have put it on the counter with these?"

Lily looked a bit taken aback, but she bravely tried to continue making conversation.

"Lovely weather out there," she said.

Mr. Morrison grunted. "Going to rain the rest of the week."

"Oh, well. It's good for the crops," said Lily, and she rang up the herbs.

When Mr. Morrison saw the total, he looked outraged.

"That's robbery, that is," he said. "That's why I never come into this place. You're nothing but a bunch of thieves."

Lily didn't reply. She waited patiently as he pulled his wallet from his pocket, counted out the money, and slapped it down on the counter.

"Thank you very much," she said. "Have a good day."

Mr. Morrison barged out of the shop with his herbs. Mom exchanged a raised-eyebrow look with Lily as she took the bread and milk to the counter.

82

"Takes all kinds," said Lily. "How are you today, Dr. Singh? Still feeding that kid, then?"

"Not for much longer," said Mom. "She's going back to the herd next week."

After lunch, Tom and Jasmine met at Willow's pen. The little goat galloped to the fence to greet them. Dad had fenced the pen so securely now that even Willow hadn't found a way to escape.

Jasmine took Sky's collar and leash out of her pocket. "You're coming for a walk," she told the goat. "Up to the town. You've done it before, but this time you'll be on a leash."

They arrived at the town green as the festival was starting. Dozens of stalls were set up around the edge of the green, with a big roped-off circle in the middle for the pet show.

"Can you see the raffle?" asked Jasmine.

Each class at the school was in charge of a stall. They had arranged with their friend Aisha, who was helping out with the raffle, to tether

Willow behind the table until it was time for the agility class.

"Hello, Willow!"

They turned to see Mrs. Thomas, wearing the same tweed skirt and shoes as last time, with another of her hand-knitted sweaters.

"Hello, dears," she said. "Lovely weather for the festival, isn't it?" She set her basket on the ground and stroked Willow's back. Willow nibbled at the empty basket.

"I wish I had something to give you, Willow," said Mrs. Thomas, "but I've just put my vegetables in the produce show. You

can have them after the judging, though, if that's all right with Jasmine."

"Of course," said Jasmine. "She loves vegetables."

"All goats do, I think," said Mrs. Thomas. "My two—" She stopped, and her cheerful face looked sad for a moment. Then she smiled brightly at the children. "If you come to the cake stall later," she said, "I'll save you some of my Victoria sponge."

"Thank you," said Jasmine. "That would be lovely. Are you coming to watch the pet show?"

"I wouldn't miss it for the world," said Mrs. Thomas. "It's my favorite part of the festival."

"We're entering Willow in the agility class," said Jasmine. "As a surprise for our parents."

Mrs. Thomas smiled in delight. "Oh, how lovely. I'm sure she'll be marvelous."

"Oh, no, there's my mom," said Tom. "We need to hide Willow."

"You take her to the raffle table," said Jasmine, "and I'll take your mom to the produce tent to see my mom." She turned to Mrs. Thomas. "We'll see you at the pet show, then."

"You certainly will," said Mrs. Thomas. "I can't wait."

10
Good Luck, Tom

Tom's mom was walking across the green, holding the guinea pigs' traveling case.

"Hello, Miss Mel," said Jasmine. "Come and see Mom's vegetables."

"Do you know where Tom is?" asked Miss Mel.

"He's over there," said Jasmine, pointing in the opposite direction from the raffle. "I'll go and tell him you're here. I think Mom would like to see you. She's a bit nervous about her entries."

She led Miss Mel to the big white tent where

the flowers and produce were displayed on long rows of tables. Mom was arranging her carrots in a perfect fan shape on a paper plate. She smiled at Jasmine and Miss Mel, and then sighed as she gazed at the carrots.

"They looked really impressive on the kitchen table," she said, "but these ones next to them are double the size. And I don't have a chance at the heaviest squash. I'm pleased with my runner beans, though. I think they're the straightest of the bunch. What do you think?"

"They look lovely," said Miss Mel. "Which potatoes are yours?"

Mom pointed them out, and Miss Mel admired their size and shape. Then she read the entry card next to Mom's plant pots. "'Two potted herbs, grown from seed.' Wow, you grew basil and coriander from seed? I can't even keep the supermarket ones alive."

"I'll go and find Tom," said Jasmine. "We'll meet you at the show ring."

88

She hurried to the raffle table, but she couldn't see Tom or Willow anywhere.

"Hi, Aisha," she said. "Have you seen Tom?"

"He's right here," said Aisha. "Your goat is so cute."

Jasmine leaned over the table and saw Tom crouching down, stroking Willow and grinning.

"So you didn't see us," he said. "That's good. Willow will be nicely hidden."

"Thanks for looking after her, Aisha," said Jasmine.

"Do I have to feed her or anything?" asked Aisha.

"No, she'll be fine. We'll come and get her just before her class."

As they walked toward the show ring, Jasmine heard somebody shouting her name. She turned to see Manu waving frantically from his stall.

"Come and have a try!" he called.

Manu and Ben were sitting at a small table behind an enormous jar of sweets. A handwritten

poster taped to the front of the table read GUESS THE NUMBER OF CANDIES IN THE JAR!

Jasmine took some change out of her pocket and handed it to Manu. She scrutinized the jar. There were all kinds of different candy inside, of all different sizes. She started to count them.

Tom gave his money to Ben and looked thoughtfully at the jar, his eyes narrowed.

"Are they the same kind of candy all the way through?" he asked. "Or did you put different ones in the middle?"

"What do you mean?" asked Ben.

"Well, you might have hidden lots of tiny ones in the middle, as a trick."

"Oh," said Manu, looking disappointed. "That would have been a really good idea."

"What if nobody guesses the right number?" asked Jasmine, who had lost count.

"Then the closest guess wins," said Ben.

Jasmine started counting again. She really wanted to win. She was hardly ever allowed to buy candy. Mom was really strict like that.

"Do you actually know how many there are?" asked Tom.

Manu and Ben shot each other a guilty look.

"Well, we did," said Manu. "The teacher wrote it down. But we might have eaten one or two."

"Manu!" said Jasmine. "How will you know who won?"

"It's OK," said Ben, pointing to the paper tablecloth. There were felt-tip pen dots all over it. "Every time we eat one, we make a dot on the tablecloth," he said. "So at the end, we'll add up all the dots and take them away from the total."

"Ben's really good at math," said Manu proudly, taking off the lid and helping himself to a lollipop.

"Stop eating them!" said Jasmine. "That's my prize you're eating."

"You haven't entered yet," said Ben.

The announcer's voice crackled through the loudspeakers. *Ladies and gentlemen, the pet show will be starting in five minutes. All entrants for the small animal class, please make your way to the show ring now.*

"We need to go," said Tom. "Put down four hundred and twenty-one for me."

"Three hundred and sixty-five for me," said Jasmine, and they ran toward the ring.

Miss Mel was waiting by the ropes, the guinea pigs' case at her feet.

"Hi, Mom," said Tom. He knelt down and opened the case.

"Wow," said Jasmine as Tom lifted Snowy out. "He looks even whiter than usual."

"I gave them a bath this morning," said Tom, handing Snowy to Jasmine while he took out his orange guinea pig, Twiglet.

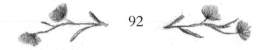

Jasmine stroked Snowy's thick, soft fur. "They'll definitely win," she said, "if that judge knows anything about animals."

Mom came hurrying across the green just as a man in a white coat with a badge saying STEWARD unhooked the rope at the entrance to the ring and asked the contestants to come in.

"Good luck, Tom," said Jasmine. "Good luck, Snowy and Twiglet."

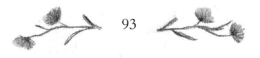

11
She's Gone

There were all kinds of pets in the small animal class: rabbits, hamsters, parakeets, gerbils, a beautiful chinchilla, and a pair of goldfish in a bowl. The owners stood in a circle, holding their pets. The judge looked at each animal in turn, inspecting their eyes and ears, looking at their feet, and asking the owners about their feeding and care.

When the judge finally came to Tom, Jasmine watched her closely, trying to read her thoughts.

She definitely looked impressed by his answers to her questions. Jasmine wasn't surprised. There was nothing Tom didn't know about guinea pigs.

After the judge had spoken to everyone, she walked to the far side of the ring and had a hushed conversation with the stewards. Jasmine bit her lip anxiously, eager to hear the judge's decision.

Then a steward handed the judge a microphone and she walked to the middle of the ring. Jasmine waited nervously as she awarded third prize to a beautiful long-haired hamster and second prize to the gorgeous fluffy chinchilla.

"And finally," said the judge, "first prize goes to Tom Hadley and his beautiful guinea pigs, Twiglet and Snowy. Congratulations, Tom!"

Jasmine clapped wildly and whooped in delight as a beaming Tom stepped forward. His arms were full of guinea pigs, so the judge pinned the ribbon to his T-shirt.

 95

"Well done, Tom! I knew you'd win," said Jasmine as he came out of the ring.

Tom's mom ruffled his hair. "Well done, Tom," she said. "I'm so proud of you."

"Congratulations," said Jasmine's mom. "Very well deserved."

"I'll take these two prizewinners home, then," said Miss Mel as Tom put the guinea pigs back in the case. "I'll be back later, Tom. I'm looking forward to seeing your trophy, Nadia."

Jasmine's mom laughed. "Not much chance of that, I'm afraid. Derek Morrison's bound to win again."

The entrants for the obedience class were waiting outside the ring. The loudspeaker crackled again. *Next in the show ring will be the obedience class, followed by agility. All entrants for the agility class, please make your way to the show ring now.*

"We'll be back in a minute," Jasmine told her mother.

"Jasmine! Tom!" came a shout.

96

Jasmine turned to see Aisha dashing toward them, a look of panic on her face.

"Willow escaped!" she cried.

"Escaped?" said Jasmine, her stomach turning over in horror.

"Willow, escaped?" said Mom, with a look of alarm. "Where is she?"

Jasmine was saved from answering by the appearance at Mom's elbow of a large, commanding-looking woman, holding a small fluffy dog.

"Dr. Singh," she said. "You treated my dog last week. I've got a couple of questions for you."

Jasmine and Tom pulled Aisha a safe distance away. "What happened?" asked Jasmine. "Where did she go?"

"I don't know," said Aisha. "Tons of people came to the raffle all at once, and I was really busy helping them, and when they went away I noticed Willow wasn't there anymore. I'm so sorry. I've looked all over the field."

97

"Did you look in the produce tent?" asked Tom.

"No, not yet."

The produce tent, thought Jasmine. *Of course.*

The three children raced through the crowds and burst through the canvas flaps of the tent. Inside, all appeared to be ordered and peaceful. The judges, a tall woman and a short man, were standing at the far end with their backs to the children, having an earnest discussion.

And then Jasmine saw Willow. She was standing by a table at the side of the tent, munching her way through a plate of runner beans.

Aisha started to run toward her, but Jasmine grabbed her arm. She put a finger to her lips and pointed to the judges.

"Shh," she whispered. "Don't startle her."

Keeping a wary eye on the judges' backs, the children tiptoed toward Willow, who had finished the runner beans and moved on to the carrots.

They crept past the plates of cucumbers and spring onions. They were almost within touching distance of her now. Jasmine was preparing to reach out and catch her when Aisha made a sudden grab at Willow's back leg.

"Yes!" she hissed.

But Willow kicked her leg free of Aisha's grasp and bolted across the tent. The judges wheeled around and stared, frozen in shock, as she crashed into the flimsy table where the trophies were displayed, knocking it over and sending the ornate silver cups clattering to the ground. Panicked by the noise, the little goat skittered out through the canvas flaps and into the crowd.

"I'll get her!" called Jasmine. And, hastily apologizing to the open-mouthed judges, she dashed out of the tent.

 99

Willow was racing through the crowd. People were pointing, laughing, and jumping out of the way. The children chased after her, but they were bigger and less nimble than she was, and it was harder for them to weave their way through the throng. And Willow was heading right toward the show ring.

"I'll go around the edge and head her back,"

shouted Tom over his shoulder as he sprinted past Jasmine. "Grab her when she comes past you."

"Excuse me, excuse me," Jasmine gasped as she elbowed, ducked, and dived through the crowds. Willow leaped right over a cocker spaniel and jumped onto the back of somebody's golden retriever. As the startled dog broke into a run, Willow rode along on its back for a few seconds

before springing off and dashing into the throng again.

Suddenly, Tom appeared on the other side of Willow. He made a grab for her but she swerved away from him. To Jasmine's horror, she bolted straight back toward the produce tent. As Jasmine raced after her, she saw her mother striding toward them. The look on her face made Jasmine's blood freeze in her veins.

12

A Menace to Society

When Tom and Jasmine ran into the tent and cast their eyes around for Willow, she was nowhere to be seen. The trophies stood upright on their table. The judges had finished inspecting the entries and were filling in names on the prize certificates. They looked up as the children entered.

"She must have gone somewhere else," muttered Tom. "Come on."

But as they turned to leave, Mom appeared in the doorway, her face furious.

"Where is she?" she demanded.

A cry of outrage came from behind them. Mr. Morrison barged his way past the gaggle of people drifting into the tent.

"Where are my runner beans? What the heck's been going on here?"

Everyone stared at him as he gazed wildly around. "My herbs!" he cried. "What's happened to my herbs?"

Jasmine looked at the table where the pots of herbs were displayed. Mr. Morrison's entry card had a FIRST PRIZE sticker attached to it. But one of his pots was overturned on the table, with the soil spilling out of it, and there were no others to be seen. Jasmine's eyes followed a little trail of soil across the floor. The trail disappeared under a table.

Mr. Morrison had obviously noticed the trail, too. He strode across and lifted the long white tablecloth. And there, nibbling at the few remaining stalks in a pot labeled PARSLEY, stood Willow.

104

The judges gasped. Some of the onlookers giggled. Mr. Morrison snatched the pot away with a roar. "I don't believe it! That blasted goat again!"

Willow tried to dash away, but Mom grabbed her and held her firmly under one arm.

"I'm so sorry," she said. "I'm really, really sorry."

"This is an absolute disgrace!" thundered Mr. Morrison. "That goat should be put down. It's a menace to society."

"It's most unfortunate, I agree," said the steward, "but it could have been worse. The entries have all been judged, and I'm delighted to say that you've been awarded the Montgomery Cup for the most prizes in the whole show, Mr. Morrison."

A glimmer of satisfaction appeared on Mr. Morrison's angry red face.

Jasmine looked at the few sorry stalks in the pot he was holding, and suddenly a thought struck her.

"Wait a minute," she said. "Didn't you buy a pot of parsley at the farm store this morning?"

A look of confusion came over his face. There were murmurs from the onlookers. Mr. Morrison gave a short, uncomfortable laugh.

"Don't be ridiculous. You must be thinking of someone else."

"No, it was definitely you," said Jasmine. "You bought a pot of parsley and a pot of thyme." She turned to the judges. "You can ask Lily at the store if you like. She'll remember. Mr. Morrison was really rude to her."

Mr. Morrison's face turned purple. He shot a brief glance at his other potted herb, overturned on the table. Jasmine followed his gaze. The entry card said: THYME. GROWN FROM SEED.

A small crowd had gathered to watch the scene. The judges were looking at Mr. Morrison in horror.

"Is this true?" asked the steward. "Did you buy these herbs?"

There was a moment of total silence. Then Mr. Morrison shouted, "Of course I didn't. This is a

107

disgraceful accusation. This whole show is a complete shambles. I'll never be entering again, you can be sure of that."

He stormed out of the tent. The crowd burst into excited chatter. The judges looked at each other with raised eyebrows.

"Is this really true?" the short judge asked Mom.

Mom nodded. "I didn't think anything of it at the time, but yes, he did buy a pot of parsley and a pot of thyme at the farm store this morning. We were behind him in line."

There was a long pause. Then the tall judge said, "Well, I don't think we'll be seeing him at the produce show again."

"That will be no loss," said the other judge. "He's been a thorn in our side for years. Always manages to find something to complain about, even when he's scooping up all the prizes." He turned to Jasmine. "I think you've done us a favor, young lady. But try not to let your goat loose in the produce tent in the future, please?"

The steward picked up Mr. Morrison's entry card and tore it in half. Then he picked up Mom's card, which bore a SECOND PRIZE sticker.

"Congratulations, Dr. Singh," he said. "Your herbs now win first prize."

"Well done, Mom," said Jasmine as the steward turned to speak to somebody else.

"Thank you," said Mom. She took a deep breath. "And well done to you, for putting two and two together. What a horrible man. It makes me wonder about all those other times he's won the trophies. I wonder how long he's been buying his prize vegetables at the farm store."

She stroked Willow's head as she spoke. Jasmine noticed the gesture and glanced at Tom, who had clearly seen it, too.

"It was all thanks to Willow," said Jasmine. "If she hadn't eaten his parsley, I'd never have noticed."

"I still don't understand how she escaped, though," said Mom. "Dad assured me he'd made that pen safer than a high-security prison."

Jasmine and Tom looked at each other.

"She didn't exactly escape," said Jasmine. "We . . . we kind of entered her in the agility class."

Mom stared at her. "You what?"

"It was a surprise," said Jasmine. "We hoped when you saw how good she was, you'd be proud of her and you might change your mind about keeping her."

"Oh, did you?" said Mom. "Honestly, Jasmine, I can't believe—"

"She's really good at agility," said Jasmine, desperate to stop Mom from going into one of her full-blown rants. "We've spent a lot of time training her. And when we entered her, the lady on the phone said they were delighted to have a goat in the competition. They've never had one before. And Mrs. Thomas is coming to watch," she added, knowing how fond her mom was of the old lady. "She loves Willow and she's really looking forward to seeing her in the agility class. You wouldn't want Mrs. Thomas to be disappointed, would you?"

An announcement came over the loudspeaker. *Could the final entrant in the agility class please come*

to the show ring now? The class is about to start and we're just waiting for Willow the baby goat. Ladies and gentlemen, for the first time ever we have a goat entering the agility competition. Come along and watch what promises to be a highly entertaining display.

Jasmine and Tom looked at Mom. Mom said nothing for a while. Then she heaved a huge sigh.

"All right," she said. "She can do the agility class. But you'd better not let her cause any more havoc, Jasmine. And you can forget about me changing my mind. It's not going to happen. Willow is going back to Mr. Evans next week."

"I know," said Jasmine. "Thank you, Mom."

But as they hurried across to the show ring, Jasmine kept her fingers firmly crossed. Once Mom saw how good Willow was in the agility class, then surely she would change her mind. Wouldn't she?

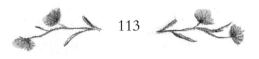

13
The Agility Class

Mom went and joined Mrs. Thomas to watch the competition, while Jasmine, Tom, and Willow stood at the end of the line of dogs and their owners waiting to go into the show ring.

The agility course began with three jumps of varying heights. Then there was a plastic play tunnel, a seesaw made from a long narrow plank balanced on a wooden barrel, and a hoop mounted vertically on two poles, for the animals to jump through. After that, there was another tunnel, then a row of thin white poles stuck into the ground, which the animals had to weave in and out of. The course ended with a final jump, the highest of all.

Jasmine and Willow had practiced all these challenges, but not in exactly this sequence. Would Willow be thrown off by having to do them in a different order?

Jasmine's biggest worry, however, was not the course, but the spectators. How would Willow react if the crowd was noisy? Would she freeze? Would she bolt?

The first dog in the ring was a silky-haired collie. His owner ran in front of him to encourage him, but he didn't seem to need encouragement. He cleared the first three jumps with ease and scampered through the tunnel. He raced up the seesaw, but when he got to the midpoint and the plank began to tip, he lost his balance, fell off the side, and tumbled head over heels on the grass. The crowd laughed as he got up, shook himself off, and, wagging his tail happily, jumped

115

through the hoop. He ran right past the second tunnel instead of going through it, but he wove his way perfectly through the slalom poles. He cleared the highest jump gracefully and finished to a burst of applause.

"He's going to be hard to beat," said Tom. "I hope they're not all as good as him."

Next in the ring was a fluffy white bichon frise. He managed the first two jumps, but when he got to the third one he just ran underneath it. He scampered through the tunnel and enjoyed the seesaw, but he refused to jump through the hoop, even when his owner tried to tempt him through with a treat. He raced through the second tunnel but totally ignored the slalom poles. He then ran underneath the final jump and out of the ring, bouncing happily and wagging his tail.

"Willow will definitely beat him anyway," murmured Tom.

Jasmine said nothing. She picked up Willow and held her close.

The third con-
testant was a gor-
geous silver pug.
Her owner led
her into the ring
to a chorus of
adoring noises
from the crowd.
This was clearly
too much for the poor pug. She turned around
and strained at her leash, desperate to leave this
strange, overwhelming place. Her owner picked
her up and tried to reassure her, but as soon as
she put her down again, the dog bolted for the
exit. After a few unsuccessful attempts to get her
to start the course, the owner shrugged, spread
out her palms apologetically to the crowd,
picked up the pug, and left the ring to a burst of
sympathetic applause.

117

"What if Willow does that?" Jasmine said anxiously to Tom.

Tom laughed. "Willow? She loves doing obstacle courses."

"Yes, but she's never done one in front of a crowd before. She might get stage fright."

The next dog to come into the ring was a border terrier, a bundle of energy who clearly couldn't wait to get going. She strained impatiently at the leash, wagging not just her tail but her entire back end in her enthusiasm.

"She might be good," said Jasmine. "Watch her carefully, Willow."

The owner bent down to unclip the terrier's leash. The dog shot off around the edge of the ring. The owner tried to call her back, but she completely ignored both him and the obstacles. She was having far too much fun racing around the ring.

Around and around she went, running at full speed, to the delight of the spectators. Her owner

tried to run after her, but when the dog saw him coming, she bolted out under the ropes and through the laughing crowd. Her poor owner, calling apologies, ran out the exit and set off in pursuit of his dog.

Several more dogs attempted the course, with varying degrees of success. Some were better at the jumps, and some at the seesaw or the slalom poles, but all of them stumbled over at least one of the challenges. As Willow's turn drew nearer, the silky-haired collie was still the one to beat.

As the final dog left the ring to a round of applause, Jasmine felt sick with nerves.

"Good luck," said Tom. "She'll be great."

"And finally," said the announcer, "we have what you've all been waiting for, our youngest competitor with our youngest handler. It's Jasmine Green and Willow the kid!"

As Willow trotted happily into the ring beside Jasmine, there was a huge burst of applause, laughter, and cries of "Ah, so cute!"

Startled by the unfamiliar sounds, Willow stiffened. Was she going to bolt?

Jasmine crouched down beside her and held her firmly around the middle.

"Don't worry, Willow," she whispered. "They're all friendly people. Just have fun, like you do at home."

She didn't dare release the little goat in case she bolted, so she continued talking softly to her, trying to reassure her. Some of the spectators seemed to sense that they were making Willow nervous, because a few people started making shushing noises. Gradually the sound died down to a murmur and Jasmine felt the goat relax.

"OK, Willow," she whispered. "Let's go."

She stood up and moved a few paces in front of the goat. She had Willow's favorite treats in her pocket, but she was hoping not to need them. In high-level agility competitions, she had learned, animals were expected to perform without the treat temptation.

 120

"Sit, Willow," she commanded, giving the hand signal.

Willow sat. There was a murmur of surprise and suppressed excitement from around the ring. Jasmine shot the spectators a reproachful look, and they quieted down.

Jasmine moved to the far side of the three jumps.

"Come on, Willow," she called.

Willow continued to sit.

"Come on, Willow," called Jasmine again.

Willow didn't move.

Oh, no, thought Jasmine. The poor little goat had frozen completely. She was petrified in these strange surroundings with a crowd of people all around her. She wasn't going to be able to do anything.

Jasmine felt guilty and angry with herself. Willow was too young for agility competitions. She shouldn't have put her through this. It had been a selfish idea.

Willow gave a little bleat. Sympathetic noises rippled through the crowd. And suddenly Jasmine's guilt and anger turned to indignation. They were sorry for her! They thought Willow wasn't going to do anything. They thought she was just a sweet little novelty act.

How dare they feel sorry for her! She would show them. She and Willow would show them what a goat could really do.

Jasmine pulled a handful of sunflower seeds and raisins from her pocket.

"Come on, Willow!" she called, opening her palm to reveal the treats.

It worked like magic. Seeing the treats, Willow sprang over the lowest jump with no effort at all, leaped over the second, and cleared the third with plenty of room to spare. As Jasmine ran to the far end of the tunnel, she heard gasps of admiration from the crowd.

Willow scrambled through the tunnel in seconds and ran straight up the seesaw. As she reached the midpoint, the seesaw began to tip. Willow paused, teetering on the narrow plank.

"Come on," called Jasmine. "Good girl, come on."

Willow took a couple of steps. The seesaw tipped right to the ground, and she ran straight down it.

"Well done, Willow," said Jasmine, running to the far side of the hoop. Willow leaped through the hoop with perfect ease. The spectators murmured in appreciation as she raced through the second tunnel.

As she got to the first slalom pole, Willow hesitated. The crowd held its breath. Jasmine ran to the far end of the poles.

"Come on, Willow," she said. "You know how to do this. We've practiced so many times. Come on."

Willow looked at Jasmine and bleated. Then she did a joyful little sideways leap and began to weave her way between the poles.

Through the poles she weaved, in and out, not putting a foot wrong. As she reached the end, Jasmine ran past the final hurdle, the high jump that had defeated so many of the dogs.

 124

"Come on, Willow," she called, holding the treats up high. "This is the last one. Up you come."

And without a second's hesitation, Willow sprang from the ground and cleared the jump, landing on the other side at Jasmine's feet.

The spectators went wild. They cheered and whooped and whistled and threw their hands in the air and jumped up and down in delight.

The only person not moving was Jasmine. She stood at the edge of the ring, holding the little goat tightly to her, stroking her soft, warm coat.

"Well done, Willow," she whispered. "You were amazing."

14
The Beginning

It didn't take long for the judge to make up her mind. When the owners and their animals had all assembled in the ring, she presented the owner of a handsome golden retriever with the third prize ribbon, and the collie with second prize.

"And now, for the first time in the history of the pet show," she announced, "I'm delighted to award first prize in the agility class to the one contestant who completed the course absolutely flawlessly. Ladies and gentlemen, a huge round of applause, please, for Jasmine Green and the wonderful Willow!"

Jasmine couldn't stop smiling as she came out of the ring with the first place ribbon in her hand.

"That was amazing," said Tom, crouching down to stroke Willow. "You totally aced it, Willow."

Jasmine felt a hand on her shoulder and looked around to see Mom, who gave her a hug.

"Well done, Jasmine," she said. "And you, too, Tom. That was incredible. You must have trained Willow fantastically well. Especially those slalom poles. It takes a long time to train an animal to do that."

"We watched lots of training videos," said Tom, "so we knew how to do it. And Willow is extremely clever."

"She certainly seems to be," said Mom. "She must be a very quick learner."

Jasmine glanced at her mother. There would never be a better time.

 128

"Don't you think it would be a terrible waste of her talents," she said, "for Willow to go into a milking herd? I mean, you wouldn't do that to a dog, would you? And you just saw that Willow's a hundred times cleverer than most dogs."

Mom smiled. "Nice logic, Jasmine, but you know it's not as simple as that. Willow may be cute and dog-size at the moment, but she'll grow to be bigger than all those dogs. And besides, it wouldn't be fair to keep her in that pen on her own forever. Goats need company."

"She could live with the sheep," said Jasmine.

Mom raised her eyebrows. "And escape every day and follow you to school? She'd find her way out of the sheep field in no time. Dad can't make every fence on the farm goat-proof, you know."

"She could live in the orchard with Truffle," said Jasmine. "Then she'd be right by the house."

Mom sighed. "Oh, Jasmine, you never give up, do you?"

"No," said Jasmine. "I don't. So what do you think?"

Mom hesitated. "You've got a real talent for agility training, that's very clear," she said. "And she does respond extremely well to you." She paused. Jasmine crossed her fingers tightly and glanced at Tom. He looked excited.

"Oh, Jasmine, that was wonderful," said a voice behind them. "Wasn't Willow extraordinary?"

Jasmine turned to see Mrs. Thomas smiling at her.

"Hello, Mrs. Thomas," she said. "You agree that goats make lovely pets, don't you?"

"Oh, they do," said the old lady. "Has your mom changed her mind, then? Willow will be a fantastic pet. I couldn't believe the way she did that agility course. She was incredible."

She stroked Willow's head, and the little goat nibbled her hand. Jasmine stole a glance at her mother. *Had* she changed her mind?

"She really is the most wonderful little

130

character," said Mrs. Thomas. "She reminds me very much of my Poppy."

"How are your goats at the moment?" asked Mom.

A shadow of sadness passed across the old lady's face. "I've just got the one now, I'm afraid. Poppy died two weeks ago. I miss her terribly, and so does Bluebell. I must go home now, actually. I only stayed to see  Willow in the agility class. Bluebell doesn't like to be left alone for too long. She gets so lonely by herself."

Mrs. Thomas stroked Willow's ears, and

Jasmine saw that there were tears in her eyes. Suddenly, she had a thought. It came so unexpectedly and felt so right that she started to speak before she could change her mind again.

"Mrs. Thomas," she said, "would you like to have Willow?"

The old lady looked at her with a bewildered expression. "Have Willow? But she's yours."

"I can't really keep her," said Jasmine. "I'd love to, but it wouldn't be fair to her. I'm at school all day, and she needs another goat to keep her company. If you had her, she'd get lots of attention, and Bluebell wouldn't be lonely anymore."

Mrs. Thomas looked adoringly at Willow. Then she said, "That's extraordinarily kind of you, Jasmine. I'm quite overwhelmed. But I couldn't possibly take this little goat away from you."

"We'd love you to have her," said Jasmine, "if you'd like to. Wouldn't we, Mom?"

Mom put her arm around Jasmine. "I think it's

the perfect solution," she said, giving Jasmine an approving glance. "Jasmine's been worried about Willow going into a milking herd, where she wouldn't get any individual attention. You'd give her the best home a goat could ever have."

Mrs. Thomas's face looked as though it had been lit up from inside. "Oh, I would love her," she said. "I would absolutely love her. And Bluebell would love her, too." She turned to Jasmine. "That's so very, very kind of you, dear. What an incredibly thoughtful thing to do."

Mrs. Thomas stroked Willow's ears, and Willow gave a little bleat. A lump rose in Jasmine's throat. While Mom and Mrs. Thomas were talking, Jasmine slipped away across the green and between the trees that fringed the town pond.

Tom found her sitting underneath a weeping willow, red-eyed and silent, her knees huddled to her chest. He sat beside her and they gazed out across the pond at the ducks.

133

"I can't believe she's going," Jasmine said eventually. "I'm going to miss her so much."

"I know," said Tom. "I really thought we'd be able to keep her."

Jasmine thought of Willow's empty shed, and tears came to her eyes again. She wiped them away as a voice sounded over the loudspeaker.

Could all prizewinners collect their prize money from the stewards' tent, please?

"That's us," said Tom. "Come on."

"Do you know how much money we get?" asked Jasmine.

Tom shook his head. "I've never won a prize before."

As they walked to the stewards' tent, Jasmine heard somebody calling her name. She turned to see Mrs. Thomas, holding the huge jar of candy from Manu's stall.

"My guess was the closest!" she said. "And I wondered if you'd like the candy. As a little thank-you for giving me Willow. It must be very hard for you to let her go."

"Oh, wow, thank you so much," said Jasmine, beaming as Mrs. Thomas handed her the jar. "That's so kind of you."

"And I want you both to come and visit Willow whenever you like," said Mrs. Thomas. "I'm just up the road, and I always keep a tin full of chocolate cookies."

"Thank you," said Jasmine. "That would be lovely."

 135

A woman waved to Mrs. Thomas and she walked over to speak to her. Tom and Jasmine joined the line of people waiting to collect their prize money at the stewards' tent. Jasmine felt a hand on her shoulder. She turned around to see her mother, with Willow on her leash.

"I'm very proud of you two," Mom said. "You've made an old lady incredibly happy. Do you realize, this is the first time you've rescued an animal and not kept it yourselves? Rehoming animals is often the hardest part of the job, and you've just done it for the first time. Well done, both of you."

Jasmine looked at Mrs. Thomas and thought what a happy life Willow was going to have, with another goat to keep her company and somebody to fuss over her every day. She thought how satisfying it was to find the perfect home for an animal, even though it was sad at the same time.

This is not the end of the story, she thought. *This is the beginning. This is where our lives as animal rescuers really start.*

They were at the front of the line now. Tom gave their names to the steward. She rifled through a tin full of brown envelopes.

"Congratulations," she said, handing them an envelope each. "Don't spend it all at once."

Tom and Jasmine thanked her, then walked away from the tent and ripped their envelopes open.

"Wow!" said Jasmine, looking over at Tom.

Tom held up his prize money and grinned at her.

"Hey, do you remember the last time we had money to spend at a fair?"

Jasmine smiled. "So," she said, "what animal should we buy this time?"

Turn the page for
an interview with Jasmine and
a sneak peek of the next book in the
JASMINE GREEN RESCUES series!

A Q&A with Jasmine Green

What are goats like as pets?

Goats can make good pets as long as you have plenty of land for them. They are social herd animals, so you need to keep at least two together, and they should be from the same herd, so they get along. They are very active and playful, so they need a lot of space, with interesting places for them to explore, climb, and investigate safely. They eat a lot, too, so they're not cheap to keep! Goats can be destructive and loud, and they are great at escaping, so you will need strong fences. You also need a shelter for them because they can't be outdoors in the rain. If you can provide all these things and give them plenty of attention, goats are friendly and fun pets. I love feeding them by hand—they gobble up banana peels and apple cores!

How well can goats really jump?

Mountain goats are the best jumpers. They can jump up to twelve feet off the ground in a single bound! Most goats can jump about four to five feet, and the kids tend to jump more than the adults. Goats are also amazing at climbing.

Do you have advice to help me train my pet to jump?

The main thing is to make the training fun for both you and your pet. Before you start, make sure your pet can follow basic obedience commands, such as Sit, Stay, and Come. When you're ready to start training, you can make a simple jump from a stick balanced on two piles of books. Then you can teach your pet to jump over the pole. First, let your pet sniff the jump so they feel comfortable with it. Then ask them to sit and stay, facing the jump. Once you've done that, get them to jump over it with you. Give them lots of praise when they do it. If they don't want to jump, try making the jump lower until they're comfortable with it. If you need help, there are some good training videos online—ask an adult to help you find one!

How many animals do you have now?

I have my two cats, Toffee and Marmite, who live in the farmhouse and roam around the yard. My collie, Sky, lives in the house, too, and he spends a lot of time outdoors helping my dad with the sheep. Out on the farm, I have Button the duck, who lives with the chickens, and Truffle the pig, who lives in the orchard and sleeps in a kennel with my dad's old spaniel, Bramble. I also have a lamb called Lucky. He lives with the other sheep in the fields, but he always comes to me for a cuddle when I call him. Willow the goat has gone to live with a lovely lady whose own goat needed company. Willow is having a great time in her new home, and luckily it's very close to Oak Tree Farm, so I can visit her every week.

Jasmine Green Rescues
A Donkey Called Mistletoe

1

The Back End of a Donkey

Jasmine and her best friend, Tom, were in the kitchen at Oak Tree Farm when Jasmine's little brother, Manu, flung the door open and ran in, dropping his coat and schoolbag on the floor.

"Guess what!" he said, an enormous grin on his face.

"What?" asked Jasmine, glancing up from the chopping board. She was cutting up a carrot as a treat for Dotty, the pet deer she had recently rescued and adopted. Dotty only had three legs, which meant she couldn't live in the wild, but she managed very well in the orchard.

"Where's Dad?" asked Manu. "I want to tell you all together."

"In his office," said Jasmine.

Their dad was the farmer at Oak Tree Farm. He worked outdoors most of the time but he had an office in the house where he did all his paperwork.

"Oh, good," said Manu, running out of the room. "I'll go get him. I've got the best news."

Jasmine's mom, Dr. Singh, walked into the kitchen and hung up her car keys. Mom was a vet, and she had picked up Manu from his after-school soccer club on her way home from the office.

"Hey, you two," she said. "I bet you're happy it's Friday."

"Yep," said Jasmine. "We're going to spend lots of time with Dotty and Truffle this weekend. Try to cheer them up."

Truffle, Jasmine's pet pig, lived with Dotty in the orchard.

"Do you think they're any better today?" asked Mom.

"No," said Jasmine flatly. "They're still lying down all the time, and they've hardly touched their food."

Until last week, Jasmine's dad's elderly spaniel, Bramble, had lived in the orchard, too. But Bramble hadn't been very well for the past few months, and on Monday she had died in her sleep.

Mom had tried to comfort Jasmine. "She was very old for a spaniel. And she had a lovely life. She got to spend every day running around the farm with Dad, and when she wasn't with him she had Truffle and Dotty to keep her company."

But Jasmine was inconsolable. She was very upset about Bramble, but she was even sadder for Truffle and Dotty. They always used to run and greet her every time she came to see them. Truffle would grunt with happiness and flop over to have

her tummy tickled. Dotty would lick Jasmine's hand and nuzzle against her. But ever since Bramble had passed, they just lay on the grass all day. Truffle kept her head down and Dotty curled herself up into a ball. They didn't even look up when Jasmine approached. Most worrying of all, they showed no interest in food.

"We're giving them carrots and grapes," Tom told Jasmine's mom. "We tried apples, but they didn't want them."

Just then, Manu came back, dragging Dad by the hand.

"So what's this amazing news, then?" asked Mom.

"We found out our parts in the annual nativity play," said Manu, "and guess what me and Ben are going to be?"

"Shepherds?" asked Mom.

Manu grinned and shook his head. "No."

"Wise men?" asked Dad.

Jasmine snorted. "Wise men? Those two? As if."

"Angels?" said Mom, and everybody laughed.

"Sheep?" suggested Tom.

Manu smiled knowingly. "Getting closer."

"Cows?" said Tom. "Pigs?"

Jasmine shook her head. "They're not clever enough to be pigs."

Manu could contain himself no longer. "We're the donkey!" he burst out.

Dad roared with laughter. "Well, that makes perfect sense."

"Mrs. Cowan's going to get an actual donkey costume," said Manu, looking as if he might burst with excitement. "Ben's going to be the front legs and the head and I'm going to be the back legs."

"Well, this is definitely an event that will need to be recorded," said Dad. "We must make sure we get front-row seats."

"We're doing a special performance for the old people at Holly Tree House the week before we do the one for the rest of the town. And we're going to have tea with the old people after the play," said Manu. "Everyone's going to sing 'Little Donkey' when me and Ben come in. Except Harrison. He won't sing. He doesn't even want to be in the play."

Harrison was a new boy in Manu's class. Manu and his best friend, Ben, had made friends with him right away. Jasmine's family had heard a lot about Harrison lately. He liked things to be calm and orderly, and he got stressed and upset if people were noisy and boisterous. So it was very strange, Jasmine thought, that Harrison would want to be friends with her brother. But the boys had bonded over a shared love of bugs, and now they seemed to spend most of their recesses making homes for insects on the school field.

"Can Harrison come over?" asked Manu. "He says there'll be lots of good bugs here, because of all the dung."

"I like the sound of Harrison," said Dad. "Not everybody appreciates the finer qualities of farm manure."

"Of course he can come," said Mom. "I'll text his mother."

"Will Ella be home in time for the play?" asked Manu. "I really want her to see it."

Ella was Jasmine and Manu's older sister, and she was away at college.

"I'm sure she'll be there if she can," said Mom. "I can't believe my son's going to be the back end of a donkey. I've never been more proud."

Which animals have you helped Jasmine rescue?

- ☐ A Piglet Called Truffle
- ☐ A Duckling Called Button
- ☐ A Collie Called Sky
- ☐ A Kitten Called Holly
- ☐ A Lamb Called Lucky
- ☐ A Goat Called Willow

About the Creators

Helen Peters is the author of numerous books for young readers that feature heroic girls saving the day on farms. She grew up on an old-fashioned farm in England, surrounded by family, animals, and mud. Helen Peters lives in London.

Ellie Snowdon is a children's author-illustrator from a tiny village in South Wales. She received her MA in children's book illustration at Cambridge School of Art. Ellie Snowdon lives in Cambridge, England.

Oak Tree Farm

Truffle found
this way

← Willow found
this way

← To village and school

Tom's
house